Freckle-
Faced

Journey of a
Young Chef

This one's for Mimi,
the original foodie who inspired us all.

www.mascotbooks.com

Freckle-Faced Foodie: Journey of a Young Chef

The author has tried to recreate events, locales, and conversations from memories of them. In order to maintain their anonymity, in some instances the author has changed the names of individuals and places.

For more information, please contact:
Mascot Books
620 Herndon Parkway, Suite 320
Herndon, VA 20170
info@mascotbooks.com

Library of Congress Control Number: 2019916320

CPSIA Code: PRFRE0220A
ISBN-13: 978-1-64543-246-3

Printed in Canada

Freckle-Faced Foodie

Journey of a Young Chef

Marlin Adams with **Ariel Fox**

Illustrations by Luiz Homero Pereira

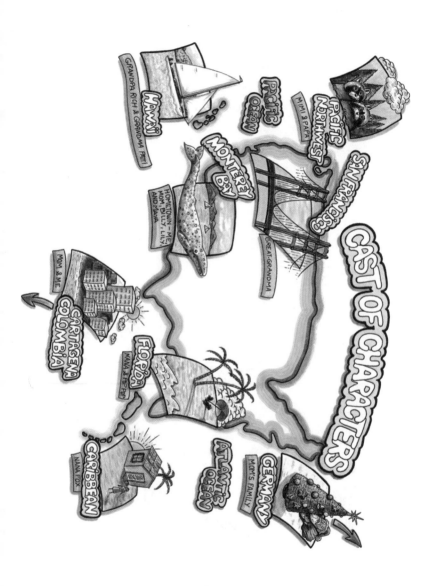

Chapter 1

What a crazy weekend. I thought it was going to do me in! The drama started on Friday afternoon . . .

"Why so gloomy?" my mom asked, noticing the frown on my face as we drove home from school.

It was a fair question—most Friday afternoons, I'm much more excited to start the weekend—even more now, with only a week to go until winter break! It's impossible to keep one single thing from Mom, especially if it has anything to do with what's going on at school. She happens to be a teacher at the very same school I go to, if you can imagine that. She is friends with all the other teachers, including my fourth-grade teacher, so I knew I wouldn't get much sympathy if I complained about what she was asking us to do.

"I was just thinking about my creative writing assignment, trying to figure out what I should write about," I replied, hoping that would be enough to satisfy her curiosity.

"Well, what's your topic?" she pressed on.

Even if I tried to change the subject, I knew she wouldn't give up until I dished out all the details. And she'd probably find out in the teachers' lounge on Monday anyway.

"We're supposed to write an essay about what our family's traditions are for the holidays, based on our culture or heritage. You know, what we celebrate, how we celebrate, what kind of special foods we eat, what songs we sing, if there are any traditions or rituals passed down from our grandparents . . . stuff like that," I explained.

"So, why do you think you're having a hard time with this topic?"

My mom has a habit of always asking me questions instead of just giving me ideas or answers. I guess that's because she's a teacher and that's what teachers love to do. What I really wanted to tell her was that I didn't feel like talking about it. Sometimes that works, but I had a feeling she wouldn't give up so easily this time—we still had another half hour in the car.

I gave in and tried to explain that I was struggling

because the way MY family celebrates the holidays isn't very interesting. Every idea I came up with was pretty boring: Christmas music, Christmas shopping, Christmas presents, Christmas trees, Christmas cookies, Christmas stockings, Santa Claus, blah, blah, blah. Even though Christmas is my favorite holiday and I love all of these activities, there was nothing that seemed interesting enough for anybody to want to read about it. Every scene that popped into my head was pretty much the standard stuff that you see on a Christmas card or on a Hallmark Christmas special.

About the only thing that might be a little unique about our holiday is the crab *cioppino* we always have on Christmas Eve with my grandparents—but I couldn't write a whole essay about crab *cioppino*!

Cultural traditions, rituals, heritage—to be honest, I wasn't exactly sure what those words even meant as they related to me. They seemed like school words. Our school is really into multicultural stuff, so we study a lot about Native American cultures, about people from other parts of the world, things like that.

This year, our principal gave each of our classrooms a different country to research. Each teacher picked a folded card from a basket to find out which country or culture to focus on with their class. They had all of us students decorate our classrooms the way the people in that country would decorate for the winter holiday. We've also been learning about traditional foods that people prepare for the holidays, and each classroom chose a recipe from "our" country to prepare and share during a school walkabout. The idea was that we'd get to experience not just Christmas or Hanukkah, but winter holidays from many different cultures and countries.

My class has been studying Sweden and St. Lucia Day, which takes place every year on December 13th. It's a celebration of this magical figure who brings light into the dark Swedish winters. From our research, it seems to be mostly about candles, gingersnaps, sweet buns shaped like sleeping cats, and *glogg,* which is a type of hot wine mixed with spices like cinnamon, cloves, ginger, orange juice, and orange peel. Our teacher obviously knew we couldn't serve spiced wine to all the kids passing through our classroom, so we made hot spiced cider instead, along with sweet buns from the biscuit dough that pops out of those twisty cans. We tried to shape the buns into cats, but they'd turned out looking kind of lame with their raisin eyes and noses and whiskers made out of pretzel sticks.

Some friends in another classroom were lucky enough to get to study Mexico. I say lucky because what they got to study and present for the walkabout was pretty much how their families already celebrate the holidays.

Which brings me back to the essay and why I seemed to be the only one stressing out about the assignment.

Before school got out that afternoon, my friends
had been hanging around together talking about ideas
they had for their essays. Their conversation included
words in Spanish that I only understood from stories
our teacher reads to us: *las posadas, la piñata navideña, el
nacimiento, los tamales.* Of course, I know what a *piñata*
is, but I'd thought they were only for kids' birthday
parties. I didn't know they were a Christmas thing as
well. I guess *el nacimiento,* which means "birth," refers
to the birth of the Baby Jesus. The only other part of the

conversation I was familiar with was making *tamales*, and that's because I sometimes go with my mom to her friends' houses to make tamales during the winter break. They call those parties *tamaladas*.

Here's the deal about my school: Almost all of the kids are of Mexican heritage. Most of the students were born here and their parents or grandparents came from Mexico, but some kids were born in Mexico and they came here with their parents who are migrant farmworkers. See, I live in a beach town, but I don't go to my neighborhood school. I commute to a school eighteen miles away from our house, since my mom teaches there. It's in a valley where they grow all kinds of fruits and vegetables, which is why many of the kids who go to my school have parents who work on the farms. Almost all of my friends are Mexican except for my Italian friend, Liliana (who we call Lily), and my friend Maya, whose dad is Guatemalan and whose mom also teaches at my school.

Pretty much all of my friends speak Spanish, even Lily, who also speaks Italian. I used to speak pretty good Spanish when I lived in South America, but once we came back to the U.S. from Colombia when I was three and a half, I told my mom I wanted to start talking "plain." That was my way of saying I didn't want to speak Spanish anymore. I don't know why I felt that way. Maybe because all of the kids in my preschool spoke English and I didn't want to feel different. It's so dumb, because now I'm struggling to learn Spanish again in school and I'm not that great at it yet.

My mom also speaks Spanish, as a bilingual teacher at my bilingual school, but she isn't Mexican. I'm not sure how to describe what she is. She always tells me she's a "mutt" and that her ancestors came from a bunch of different places in Europe, but mostly from England, Ireland, and Germany. My dad, Billy, is Black (or Afro-American, as he says), and he comes from New Jersey. He's not my biological father, but he's my "real dad" because he's the one who's really been there since I was four. My biological father, or "bio dad," is Colombian, but he's also Black (or Afro-Caribbean, as my mom describes him). He's bilingual too. He speaks Spanish, which is the language he learned in school, but his main language is a different kind of English that the locals speak on the island where he comes from. They all kind of sound like they're singing when they talk. They call it *Patois,* and it comes from a combination of English and different African languages. It started back when the English were capturing Africans and bringing them to these islands to work as slaves on the sugar plantations.

I don't see him at all anymore since we moved back from Colombia, but I still remember living down there when I was really little. The summer before third grade, I got to go back and visit his mom, my grandmother. I call her Nana Fox. She lives on one of the islands in a tiny wooden house that's built up on big cement blocks so it won't flood when the tropical rains come. Her house is painted bright pink and turquoise, and there's a fence in the front yard that's made out of these beautiful pink, pearly conch shells. I could easily write a whole story about that place, but that wasn't what my assignment was about.

I'm actually pretty lucky to have lots of grandparents in lots of different places. The funny thing is that most of them live on islands, even though the islands are all totally different.

I see my mom's parents, Mimi and Papa, the most often. They used to live in my town until they moved up to an island in the Pacific Northwest.

My Grandpa Rich lives on a big sailboat on an island in Hawaii with his girlfriend. I call her Grandma Patti, even though she's not really my grandma. Despite his name, he's not actually rich. Grandpa Rich says he's a starving artist. He's my mom's "bio dad," but she was raised by Papa, just like I'm being raised by my mom's second husband. The cool thing is that Mom and Grandpa Rich got to know each other again once she was grown, so he has been around ever since I was born.

I have two more grandparents, Nana and PopPop. They're Billy's parents and even though they don't live on an island, they live in Florida by the beach, so the weather feels just like the Caribbean.

My Papa's mother lives pretty close to us in "the city," which is what we call San Francisco. For some reason, she's the only one I call Grandma, even though she's my great-grandmother. She came here from Russia when she was very young and she doesn't remember how to speak Russian. Too bad, or I might have been able to call her *Babushka,* which is how you say "Grandma" in Russian.

I really don't know what you would call my culture. I used to tell everyone I was Mexican, because when they would ask me where I was from and I told them I was from "here," they'd say, "No, but where are you REALLY from? What ARE you?" I guess I didn't know how to explain that I'm biracial, and I didn't want to go into all the details about having two fathers and all these grandparents, so I'd just decided it was easier to say I was Mexican like pretty much everyone else I knew.

After we got home and finished dinner that night, I started thinking again about all of my grandparents and how different they all are from one another. I wondered whether there was anything special or interesting I could write about from my memories of time I've spent with them. But our Christmas traditions don't really have much to do with the most interesting things I could share about my grandparents. The images that kept popping into my head were mostly of the cool places where they live and the fun stuff we do when we're together.

One thing's for sure: we all love to eat! I thought about how much time each of my grandparents spend cooking yummy food and how much I love to eat what they cook, especially my Mimi. The thing that's special about her is that she happens to be the best cook in the world and I could probably write a whole book filled with her recipes! She also lets me cook with her all the time and she has taught me how to make lots of amazing things all by myself. The first thing she ever taught me to make was fresh basil pesto with basil right out of her garden. I like to put it on my favorite pasta, bowtie pasta.[1]

But none of that had anything to do with Christmas traditions.

---

1   It's such a great meal, I'm sure it'll be one of your favorites too. You can find my recipe for it on pages 96-97!

Chapter 2

I stayed up late, remembering back as far as I could to the time when I lived in Colombia and the Caribbean. I lived with my mom in Cartagena, Colombia from age two to three-and-a-half. We moved down there so Mom could study Spanish. She also managed a restaurant while we were there, and I went to a *colegio infantil,* which is what they call preschool in Spanish.

Even though my mom and my biological father were divorced by then, we still went on vacation a few times to visit him and my Nana Fox on the island where they lived. I remember how gorgeous and clear and sparkly the turquoise water was, how the sandy beaches were so white they almost blinded you, and how there was music playing everywhere we went—soca, salsa, calypso, and reggae, which is my favorite of all the music they play down there. Mom loves reggae music too. She actually knew Bob Marley and his family before he died, right before I was born, and she plays his albums all the time.

If music wasn't pumping from the speakers of shops, restaurants, and people's houses, it was coming live from musicians on the beach, on the street corners, or in the outdoor cafes. Mom tells me I used to get to play every day with my friends who lived right on the beach.

It was mad hot down there, but we went swimming in the ocean most days (or in the "sea," as the islanders call it), and there were always offshore breezes and afternoon tropical rain showers and lots of fans everywhere to cool us off. We drank gallons of fruit smoothies; I remember a place called *Jugolandia* where we went for my favorite juice, *jugo de maracuya*. Back then, I didn't know what that was in English, but now I know it's the same as passion fruit. I also loved to eat another funny fruit called *mamoncillo*. I've never seen those since. They look like little limes but they have this yummy, sweet, slippery fruit inside. You just bite into the skin and it pops open; you suck the big black seed out, chew the fruit off, and then spit out the seed afterwards. I ate a gazillion of those! The problem was that the juice would dribble down onto my clothes and leave a stain that my mom could never get out. She says

all of my clothes back then had *mamoncillo* stains.

There were coconut palm trees and mango trees everywhere on the island; we ate mangos and drank fresh coconut water called *agua de coco* that came from green cocos right off the tree every single day. When I went back to visit, it seemed like they made everything with coconut, like *arroz con coco* (coconut rice), *pastel de coco* (coconut pie), *leche de coco* (coconut milk), and

paletas de coco (coconut popsicles). And EVERYTHING was fried in coconut oil—the whole island smelled like it!

I have one mental image—I'm not sure if it's truly a memory or if I've just seen photographs of it—from way back when I was three. We used to go to a beach by our apartment in Cartagena where women walked up and down the shore with huge metal tubs of fresh fruit balanced on their heads and *machetes* or large knives in their hands. These women were called *Palenqueras.* Mom says that's because they originally came from San Bassilo de Palenque, a small village founded by runaway slaves and one of the first places where Africans were freed from slavery. These ladies reminded me of the photos of African women I've seen in books, walking as straight as sticks, balancing those huge baskets and tubs with fruit, water, laundry, and lots of other things on their heads.

In Cartagena, the *Palenqueras* would stop where I was playing in the sand to give me slices of watermelon, papaya, mangos and pineapple to eat—but I didn't know they weren't really just GIVING me the fruit. They would walk up to me, cut a piece of fruit, hand it to me, and then as soon as I stuck it in my mouth, they would shout over to Mom and tell her how much she owed. One time, she didn't even have the change she needed to pay the lady. We had to walk all the way back to our apartment to get the money, then all the way back to the beach where the *Palenquera* was still patiently waiting to be paid. After that day, my mom finally gave up trying to stop me from accepting pieces of fruit every time the ladies offered them to me and just started bringing change to the beach in a little coin purse. Who could resist fresh tropical fruit? And what could be a healthier snack?

It's a little curious when I look back on it, but we hardly ate any meat when we lived down there, even in the restaurant my mom managed—except at this other restaurant owned by some of our good friends from Argentina. When we went there, we ate the most amazing grilled steak with *chimichurri*, this delicious sauce made with parsley or cilantro, lots of garlic, olive oil, vinegar, and hot peppers. Mom still likes to makes that sauce whenever we barbecue steak.

We did eat TONS of fresh fish and shellfish, both

at our little apartment by the beach in Cartagena and when we went to visit the islands. All the fish and seafood had names that were either Spanish or Patois: *pargo frito* (fried snapper), *sancocho de pescado* (fish soup), *caracol* (conch), *cangrejos rellenos* (stuffed crab backs), *Ol' Wife* (fried triggerfish), and *rondón* (seafood stew with fish, conch, breadfruit, yucca, and plantains cooked in coconut milk). *Rondón* is my Nana Fox's specialty, and she cooks it over an outdoor fire made inside of a big metal drum. It's amazing that she can cook all kinds of things outdoors without an actual stove or oven in her house. She bakes these little dumpling things called Johnny cakes, *empanadas* (turnovers), and *arepas* (corn cakes) right over the fire.

They are all delicious, but my favorite is her *patacones* (fried plantains). She even taught me how to make them. First, she peels and cuts green *plátanos* (plantains) that aren't ripe yet into slices, and then soaks them in saltwater. When they are good and salty, she takes them out, dries them off, and fries them in a pan over the fire—in coconut oil, of course! After a few minutes, when they start to turn golden, she takes them

out of the pan and puts them on a sheet of newspaper to soak up the oil. The best part is when she pounds and smashes each one with the flat side of a big knife, sprinkles them with more salt, then puts them back in the pan of hot coconut oil until they are crispy and golden brown. That's when she takes them out of the pan again, soaks up some more of the oil on newspaper, sprinkles them with another pinch of salt, and serves them piping hot. They are to die for![2]

Finally getting sleepy, the last thought I had was of Nana Fox cooking her *patacones* over the fire in front of her colorful little house by the sea.

---

[2] Seriously, you have to try them for yourself—check out the recipe on pages 98-99.

Chapter 3

As soon as I woke up Saturday morning, I remembered my essay assignment and got anxious. Not one of my Colombian memories helped me describe my family's cultural traditions for the holidays. *Patacones* are definitely NOT part of our holiday meal. I still had Saturday and Sunday to think about it, but I was annoyed that I couldn't relax and enjoy my weekend until I came up with a plan.

I started thinking about how different my life has been in the U.S. since we returned from South America. A MAJOR game changer is that my mom got married again—now I have the best dad in the world. Billy always tells me that he fell in love with the two of us and how lucky he was to get such a package deal. Just thinking about him puts a smile on my face. Of course, Billy is around every day, not just Christmas, so that wasn't helpful for my essay!

I thought about my whole heap of grandparents and

whether any of them contribute something unique to our holiday traditions. We celebrate Christmas with my Mimi and Papa; even though they recently moved away, they are still coming down to spend the holidays with us like always. I got to spend three weeks with them up at their new house in the Pacific Northwest last summer, so I really haven't even had a chance to miss them too much.

My great-grandma lives an hour away, and we just drove up there a few weeks ago for Sunday dinner. We'll see her again when we make our annual Christmas shopping trip to the city. She's a great cook too, but I couldn't think of any of her recipes that have become part of our Christmas traditions.

Since my mom remarried, I gained a new set of grandparents, Nana and PopPop, who come to visit us sometimes from Florida; I also got to visit them on my way back from Colombia the summer before last, when I went to visit Nana Fox.

I counted up all my grandparents on my fingers and my grandpa in Hawaii was number seven, with "Grandma" Patti making number eight. Over the past summer, before I went up to stay with Mimi and Papa, I got to spend three weeks in the Hawaiian Islands with Grandpa Rich and Grandma Patti on his sailboat. You'd think that out of eight grandparents there would have been SOMETHING to give me a clue about my culture.

I'd taken notes and jotted down some things my teacher wrote on the board when she gave us our assignment, so I went and got my notebook to read what I had written: "Food is the most celebrated representation of culture. In every culture we all share the instinctive desire to break bread together."

As I thought about what those words meant, three categories kept circling around in my head: *place* . . . *family . . . food.*

I decided I needed to make a chart, because that's what my mom always does when she's planning her lessons. I raced down the ladder from my bedroom loft, bolted into the kitchen, and practically collided with her carrying her coffee into the living room. I stopped just in time and asked if I could borrow some chart paper and markers. (She always has huge stashes of both.) And then I escaped quickly into the family room where she keeps all of her teacher stuff before she could start nosing around about why I needed the supplies. I grabbed a whole pad of chart paper and a fresh box of markers and sneaked back the other way upstairs to my loft.

I propped the chart pad up against the wall on top of my desk, took out five new markers in black, green, red, purple, and blue, and neatly printed a heading in green at the top of the page: **Culture.** Next, I drew one horizontal line and two vertical lines with the black marker down the page to make three columns. Above the left column, in red, I wrote **Place**. Above the middle column, in purple, I wrote **Family.** Above the right column, in blue, I wrote **Food**. After drawing another horizontal line under the three sub-headings, I was ready to start filling in the columns. I'm pretty good at categorizing and classifying in school, so I knew this was going to be a cinch.

The first entries were easy because I had been thinking about my time in Colombia all Friday night; all I had to do was write down what I had been remembering. Under the **Place** heading, the first

thing I wrote, no surprise, was "Colombia." Under the **Family** heading, I put "Nana Fox." Under the **Food** heading, I listed all the scrumptious things I had been daydreaming about.

Next, I went back to the **Place** heading and jotted down a few words to jog my memory when it came time to start actually writing the essay, some descriptions of the island and of our place in Cartagena. I decided to draw another horizontal line across the page under that, so I could separate it from what I wrote next. That would help me organize my paragraphs later. My teacher (and my mom, of course) would be proud!

The next place I focused on was Hawaii, which I wrote in the **Place** column, and "Grandpa Rich" and "Grandma Patti" in the **Family** column. I started to write down some of my memories from my trip last summer.

What I like most about being in Hawaii is being on Grandpa Rich's sailboat. He lives on the boat, so that's where I stay when I go to visit. I have my own little berth, which is kind of like a cubbyhole, but long enough for a person to stretch out. It's the coziest place in the world to sleep. You can hear the waves lapping up against the hull (the side of the boat) as the gentle motion rocks you like you're in a cradle.

Grandpa Rich taught me that you always refer to a boat as "she." His boat is not a little sailboat like the ones I see out sailing on the bay by my house. She's technically a yacht, a huge old schooner—she's 80 feet long! That's longer than the distance from the front

of our house, through the living room, through the kitchen, through Mom and Billy's bedroom, and out into our backyard! She has two gigantic masts that look like telephone poles and lots of huge white sails that we hoist up when we leave the harbor so we can catch the wind and go ripping out to sea. When all the sails are up, she looks like a pirate ship. Her name is *Tradition*—hmm, as in cultural tradition, maybe? I wondered if there might be a clue there for my essay.

During my visit, we'd spent most of our days on the boat, either in the harbor or out sailing and fishing. One day, Grandpa Rich caught a wahoo fish (or *ono*, as it's called in Hawaiian). When we got back to shore, I watched him fillet it with his fishing knife, getting it ready to cook on the grill that evening for dinner. We did all of our cooking either in the galley, which is what you call a kitchen on a boat, or else we grilled on the little barbecue up on the deck. Grandpa Rich gave a big piece of the *ono* to Grandma Patti to make *poke* and he saved the rest to grill later.

I went down below (that's what you call it when you go down the companionway, the ladder into the boat from the deck) and watched how Grandma Patti prepares *poke*. First, she cuts the fish into bite-sized cubes, and then she mixes the cubes in a bowl with a little olive oil and the juice she squeezes from a lime. Next, she adds some chopped green onions, some red chili pepper flakes, some soy sauce, a little bit of sesame oil, and a bit of dried ogo seaweed—*limu*, as they call seaweed in Hawaiian.

Once she had it all mixed together, we sampled it,

and then she put it in the refrigerator to let it marinate and get cold before dinner time. I had tried raw fish before in sushi rolls, but I had never tasted anything like this. It's amazingly delicious! The grilled *ono* that we had later that night tasted just as yummy. There's nothing like fresh fish right from the ocean, whether you cook it or eat it raw!

During the day when we weren't out sailing, Grandma Patti and I usually walked to the local beach to go for a swim and sit out in the sun until we started to turn pink. Well, until she turned pink, that is. She's a redhead and can't stay out in the sun too long. I get tan super fast, and then freckles pop up all over my face. I used to call them "freckers" when I was little, so that's now one of my nicknames because I have a million freckles. (I have a few choice nicknames, but that's another story.)

After our swim, we'd head back to the boat to find Grandpa Rich. He was always either up working on the deck or painting one of his watercolors down below. He paints beautiful watercolor paintings of different kinds of boats and the ocean.

One day, I stayed with him on the boat, and he hoisted me up to the top of the mast in the bosun's chair, the little harness chair attached to the huge poles. I could see all of the other boats in the harbor, the beach, the waves breaking offshore, the palm trees along the road—even the green mountains in the distance. Now I knew why they call it a "bird's eye view." A bunch of seagulls flew right past me, and Grandpa Rich told me that they must have hitchhiked a ride on a cruise ship and followed me from California. You don't see many seagulls in Hawaii because they don't breed or raise their families there. They were just visitors, like me! It was pretty cool being up as high as the birds, and I wasn't even afraid.

My favorite outing was when we'd drive out to this big beach on the opposite side of the island, stopping on the way at a coffee house and art gallery where Grandpa Rich sells some of his paintings. We always ordered the Aloha Smoothie, a heavenly blend of fresh mango, papaya, orange juice, crushed ice and a little bit of milk. We love those smoothies so much that we figured out how to make them back on the boat so we could have them every morning. I've even kept making them since I got back home.[3]

One time after we went to the coffee house and art gallery, we decided to go to another smaller beach where Grandpa Rich said we would most likely see giant green sea turtles, which the Hawaiians call *honu*. We parked our car on the side of the road and hiked down to the spot where Grandpa Rich had seen the turtles before. We laid our towels down in the sand, put on our masks, snorkels, and fins, and swam out into the warm water.

We hadn't been in the water for more than five minutes before Grandpa Rich tapped me on the arm and pointed towards what I thought was a big rock ahead of us. My heart skipped a beat when I saw what he was pointing at. Swimming right in my direction was the biggest turtle I'd ever seen in my life! I panicked for a second, but then I remembered that he had told me how gentle and harmless they are. I attempted to just float and calmly tread water where I was, my face still

---

3 You can try them for yourself—check out the recipe on pages 100-101!

in the water, my eyes glued to the giant creature coming my way. I could hear my heart pounding in my ears.

Mr. Honu just swam right up to me, looked at me for a moment with his buggy brown eyes, and then gracefully made a turn to the right with his big flippers and continued to paddle towards the shore. I felt like I was in *The Land Before Time* or something with some kind of prehistoric creature. I couldn't believe it was real.

We continued snorkeling for about half an hour and then we headed back to the beach. We took our fins and masks off and walked back to where we had left our towels. It was already getting really hot that morning, so we decided we would sit there long enough to dry off a bit before hiking back to the car. Grandpa Rich fell asleep like he always does and I was just kind of spacing out, gazing out at the water. I glanced over to my left and had to do a double take. I couldn't believe what I saw on the beach. There he was, that giant turtle, just sunning himself the same way we were! Old Mr. Honu had come all the way ashore and was lying there in the sand.

I got up and slowly walked over in his direction to

have a closer look, trying not to make any noise and remembering that you're never supposed to touch or feed sea turtles, in or out of the water. I got within about five or six feet of him and lay down on my side in the sand so I could observe him at his level. He just ignored me and kept on sunning himself. He was about the same size as me!

I spent at least five minutes just silently watching him, afraid to move a muscle, and then I carefully got up and walked back to Grandpa Rich to wake him up and show him my discovery. He smiled and told me how lucky I was—I received a Hawaiian blessing that day. The Hawaiians believe that the *honu* are sacred; they are kind of like ancestral guardian spirits. That's my best memory from Hawaii, for sure.

As cool as it was to spend time with Grandpa Rich and Grandma Patti in Hawaii aboard *Tradition*, it's not really part of my heritage. We're not Hawaiian, even if my grandpa is called *kama'aina* by the locals, which is how they describe any long-term residents of the islands, even if they're not actually Hawaiian. As great as these experiences were, they weren't going to help me write my essay. I didn't think we'd be adding Aloha Smoothies or *ono poke* to our Christmas meal.

I sighed and added details into the three columns about the rest of my Hawaiian memories and drew another horizontal line underneath what I had written.

I was ready for a break.

Chapter 4

I went downstairs to clear my head, and I was just in time to find Mom and Billy making sandwiches for lunch. Avocado, Monterey Jack cheese, and sprouts on sourdough French bread—my favorite!

"Where have you been hiding all morning, Hogan?" Billy asked.

Hogan. Another one of my nicknames. Billy started calling me that when I was four. There used to be a comedy TV show called *Hogan's Heroes* back in the day, and Billy loves to watch the reruns. The main character, Hogan, is a colonel in the U.S. Army and a prisoner in a Nazi POW camp during World War II. In the show, he and his prisoner buddies do all kinds of crazy things to trick the Nazis. It's pretty hilarious, even though there's nothing funny about the real Nazis! Billy said Hogan has a whiny voice, so whenever I used to whine, he called me Hogan. Unfortunately, it stuck, and to this day, I'm known to my family by that name, like it or not.

My friends know better than to try and call me that, or worse, to let anyone else know it's my nickname. My actual name has enough problems. When I introduce myself, I have to say, "Ariel, and not like the antenna. Get it? Just think of these three letters: R-E-L." Nobody in Colombia ever had trouble pronouncing it correctly. I don't know why it's so difficult for people in this country!

To answer Billy's question, I replied, "I've been working on a homework assignment. I'm about to write the part where we went to Florida to visit Nana and PopPop summer before last."

"That's what your assignment is about?" he asked, kind of surprised.

"It's a long story," I replied. "I'll share it with you when I'm done. I'm kind of writing about family recipes."

I did not really want to get into the details. Besides, I was beginning to think that the whole project was probably turning out to be a big fat waste of time. None of my family recipes seemed to have anything to with our holiday traditions.

We all sat down at the little kitchen table and ate

our sandwiches. Billy asked if I wanted to go downtown to the bookstore with him, which is one of my favorite things to do. As much as I would have loved to get out of the house and away from my task, I knew I had better get back to it before the day was over.

"Thanks, but I think I'd better go back upstairs and keep working on my project."

They both looked at me like I was an alien or something.

"Who ARE you, and what have you done with our daughter?" he kidded.

My mom laughed, and then offered to go to the bookstore with him and said it would give me the house to myself to continue working in peace and quiet.

I was relieved because I really wanted to finish my essay before evening. Lily and Maya were coming over for a sleepover, and I wanted to be done so I could just hang out, not worrying about my dumb homework.

Mom and Billy said goodbye and headed for the car. I trudged back to the loft ladder, climbed up, and got back to my trip down memory lane.

I wrote "Florida" in the first column, "Nana and

PopPop" in the second, and then thought back on our trip: what it was like being there, what kinds of things we did, and of course, what kind of food we ate. Their house is close to a beach that really does look a lot like the beaches in Colombia and the Caribbean. The sand is as white as can be, the water is the same brilliant turquoise, and the shore is lined with coconut palm trees. It's totally different from the beach in my town. The water is so warm there compared to here! It's almost painful to swim in the ocean here without a wetsuit top, but when we were there, we swam every day and it wasn't hard at all to dive right into the water. It didn't take any getting used to.

What was different about Florida from Colombia or the Caribbean is that we didn't eat any fish while we were there, even though we were so close to the sea. For some reason, those grandparents like to barbecue chicken more than they like to cook fish.

When I tried to recall some of the meals we had, three things immediately popped into my head: two that were delicious, and one that was truly disgusting. My favorite memory was of the sweet potato pudding my Nana made. That, and her tasty collard greens. I've always loved spinach and chard, but until that trip, I had never tried collard greens before. I would like to learn how to make them the way she does. I did watch her make her scrumptious sweet potato pudding, and Mom and I have made it together one time since we came back home.[4]

Next, I thought about the not-so-tasty memory. One morning while we were there, I walked into the kitchen to see what PopPop was doing before anyone else was up and about. He had just finished frying some okra, and it smelled great. He had taken it out of the pan and was letting it cool down a bit on a plate next to the stove. He took out two more plates from the cupboard and divided the fried okra into two big portions, one for himself and one for me. I thanked him and sat down with him at the kitchen table, ready to dig in.

Boy, was I in for a shock! I took my first bite and almost gagged. Not only did it taste gross, but it was also the slimiest thing you could ever imagine! I spit it into my napkin on the sly, hoping he wouldn't notice.

---

4   You can too—sneak back to pages 102-103 and I'll show you how!

"Well, how is it?" he asked.

"Umm, not quite what I was expecting," I answered. "It tastes different than it smells and it's kind of slimy."

Just then, Billy walked into the kitchen and saved the day. "Oh no! You're not trying to make her eat that okra, are you?"

Phew, that was a close one. I thanked my grandpa again, excused myself from the table, and scooted out of there, leaving Billy to smooth over the situation. I don't think I'll ever try okra again. That and bananas are about the only foods I can think of that I don't like.

I wrote a few words about the beach in Florida, the collard greens and the sweet potato pudding, and the word "okra" with a sad face next to it; then I drew one more horizontal black line underneath it all.

But guess what? Still nothing to help with my essay, and I had gone through half a dozen grandparents. I only had two more to go.

I plopped down on the floor and started thinking about Mimi and Papa, my mom's mom and dad, the ones I spend the most time with. I was starting to get a little bored with my chart, but I couldn't just quit and leave them out. I wrote "Mimi and Papa" in the second column, but then I couldn't decide if I should write about where they moved, up in the Pacific Northwest, or about where they had lived most of my life, in my town.

And when it came to food, I didn't even know where to begin. Like I said, my Mimi is the best cook in the world, and she has taught me so many things in her kitchens. I think my favorite hobby or pastime is to take a bunch of separate ingredients and turn them into something yummy to eat. It's kind of like magic. You never know how it's going to turn out when you're reading or inventing your own recipe, but it's totally rad when you end up with a finished product that looks and tastes delicious.

Chapter 5

I was feeling kind of overwhelmed trying to narrow down what to write about Mimi and Papa, since my whole life is filled with memories and stories about my time with them. I had to remind myself to focus on the topic and look for some kind of connection to the holidays and our family traditions.

Food and **Place**. A million images popped into my head when I thought about cooking with Mimi. I decided to just go get my notebook and start free-writing, like my teacher has us do to "get our juices flowing."

The first thing I did was describe the backyard of Mimi and Papa's old house, because that backyard had a lot to do with the things we'd cooked, like the fresh basil pesto. I wrote about the big brick patio that Papa designed with spaces in the middle to plant things, as well as the wine barrel and redwood planter boxes that he built and placed all around the patio. In that yard, they'd had fruit trees, strawberries, tomato plants, lettuce, radicchio, green beans, zucchini plants, an herb garden, and all kinds of beautiful flowers.

Unfortunately, because Mimi is really into organic gardening and never uses sprays or pesticides, she also had an army of snails that loved to snack on those garden goodies! She got so tired of battling the snails that she decided she was going to do like the French do and turn them into *escargot*—which, if you don't know, is a famous French delicacy made from actual snails and a ton of garlic and butter. I'm totally serious. I know this because I helped her make it!

I laughed out loud, remembering the steps we had to follow to make the *escargot*. I don't know where or how Mimi learned to do this. Maybe from reading an article in *Gourmet* or *Bon Appétit,* two of her cooking magazines that I love to look at.

The first thing we did was go out into the yard with a big bucket and collect as many snails as we could find from all of their favorite garden hiding spots. Once we started dropping them in the bucket, we had to put a dish towel over the top of it to keep them from crawling out. I happen to be terrified of spiders, but I don't seem

to have an issue with any other creepy crawlers, and snails are no exception. Searching among the plants and flowers was kind of like going on an Easter egg hunt, which I'd also done many times in that backyard.

Little by little, we found all of their hiding places. They seem to like ripe and juicy strawberries just as much as I do, because I found a bunch of them gnawing away on the strawberry plants.

Once we had gathered enough snails, probably around fifty, we brought them inside and into the kitchen and carefully placed them in a big roasting pan, like the kind you use to roast turkey for Thanksgiving. Mimi put a small dish of water in the corner of the pan and then poured about a half a cup of yellow cornmeal into the other corner, along with a few sprigs of thyme from her herb garden. After that was done, she covered the pan with a piece of cheesecloth, a kind of gauzy, see-through cloth which kept the snails from crawling out and also kept them from suffocating. She tied a piece of string around the cheesecloth that hung over the edge of the pan to keep it from coming off.

Mimi explained why we were doing this: "We

have to purge the snails by putting them on a thyme and cornmeal diet. It takes a few weeks to clear their innards of any toxins, dirt, or other stuff they may have been nibbling. We'll know the purge is working once we see little yellow and green poop trails in the pan."

That part really cracked me up. But it turned out to be true!

It was summertime when we took on this project, so I was spending lots of time at Mimi and Papa's when I wasn't hanging out at my friends' houses or going to the beach. It took a few weeks of carefully taking the snails out of the pan every other day, putting them back in the bucket while we washed the pan, replacing the water, thyme, and cornmeal, and then gently placing them back in the pan. I kept thinking what a great science project this would be—predicting how long it would take for the yellow and green poop trails to come out, or which snail would be the first to make the purge— and wondering if I could do this again once I was back in school.

Finally, on one morning at the end of the second week, Mimi got this funny, kind of worried look on her face and told me it was time to move on to the next step.

"I'm sorry, honey, but now that the snails are squeaky clean on the inside, I'm afraid we have to put them in a bowl of salt, which as you can probably figure out, is going to kill them."

Even though I'd known we were eventually going to eat them, I got really sad thinking about how we had created this little snail resort just to trick them and put them into a bowl of snail kryptonite! I could honestly see why people decide to become vegetarians. If I was getting sentimental over garden snails, I couldn't even imagine what it's like for kids who live on ranches or farms and raise lambs, goats, and pigs to have to slaughter and eat them!

I could tell that Mimi was feeling a little guilty when she suggested that I have my mom pick me up and bring me back later that day to move on to the cooking stage. I took the coward's way out and left her to carry out the dirty work all by herself.

When I returned that afternoon, she had already placed the snails in the bowl of salt, which not only did them in like she'd told me it would, but also helped pull the slime from them at the same time. She had rinsed them off, and they were now ready to throw into a pot of boiling water mixed with white wine and more herbs from the garden.

We simmered them in the pot for about half an hour, then lifted them out a few at a time with a slotted spoon, watching as the last of the slime dripped off the spoon. As if that wasn't gross enough, the next thing we had to do was pry their little snail bodies out of their shells with a toothpick. We were finally ready to cook the snail meat, and I wasn't feeling that sorry for them anymore. Nothing like slime to turn you against a poor innocent creature.

Mimi tossed the snails in garlic, parsley, lemon, white wine, and, of course, butter—lots of melted butter. While they were in the pan cooking, she went to the pantry and brought out a few bags of these fancy snail shells from France. They had beautiful tan and white swirly patterns, and they were bigger than the shells that the snails used to live in.

We took the cooked snails from the pan and put one snail inside of each of the empty French shells, poured some of the melted garlic butter inside of each shell, placed the stuffed shells on two cookie sheets, and then put them in the oven to heat up until the butter was bubbling and the whole house smelled like delicious garlic butter. We divvied up the cooked snails into three bowls, poured the remainder of the garlicky butter over them, tossed up a big green salad, cut up a loaf of my favorite sourdough French bread from our local bakery, and called Papa to the table.

The three of us sat down and dug in. I was a little nervous when I took my first bite, but the garlic butter made it taste so good I forgot all about what we were actually eating. I'm now a serious fan of *escargot!*

I laughed again thinking about that experience and imagined myself traveling to France some day and bravely ordering *escargot* off the menu in some fancy French restaurant.

That was a great memory—but did *escargot* become one of our Christmas meal traditions? No, it did not. Yikes. What other dishes did Mimi cook that could be part of our holiday story besides the crab *cioppino?* Unfortunately, we never made Mimi's other specialties, like that pesto pasta made with fresh basil from her herb garden, for the holidays.

I go "foraging" with Mimi and Papa, which means finding and gathering food out in nature. Super cool and fun to do. We go down to the cliffs by the ocean at low tide to these huge mussel beds and find hundreds of mussels clinging to the rocks. We pry dozens and dozens of them off with these old butter knives that Mimi brings along for the job. We can only go during the late fall and early winter months of the year, around Halloween, because mussels are quarantined during the earlier months—you can't eat them when the ocean is warmer because they're actually poisonous!

One day after we had collected a bucketful of enough mussels to make a big family feast, we hiked back to the car and headed up the coast for home. Mimi asked Papa to pull over and stop along the way by another spot next to the ocean, close to a field where the farmworkers had finished harvesting Brussels sprouts earlier that day. We got out of the car, walked over to a spot next to the cliff, and Mimi showed us where to gather a bunch of the loose Brussels sprouts from the ground so she could roast them in the oven to go along with the mussel stew. I'm not sure that could really be considered foraging, or if we could have actually been arrested for stealing some stinky old Brussels sprouts from some guy's farm!

These memories were closer to the right season, but mussel stew and Brussels sprouts still aren't part of our traditional holiday meal.

When I came back from Hawaii this summer, I got to go spend the last three weeks of my vacation up in the Pacific Northwest at Mimi and Papa's new house. Papa is a great fisherman (probably even better than Grandpa Rich), and he also has a boat. It's totally different from Grandpa Rich's schooner, though. Papa's boat is an old classic too, but it's a power boat, not a sailboat, and it's tiny compared to *Tradition*. Papa's boat is great for fishing up in the Puget Sound, the waterways along the coast of Washington.

While I was there, Mimi and Papa and I went out fishing one day for salmon. That was sort of fun, but it was kind of boring too, just sitting on the boat waiting for Papa to hook a salmon. It wasn't as exciting as deep-sea fishing in Hawaii with Grandpa Rich, and it wasn't nearly as fun as when I go freshwater fishing in creeks and rivers with Mimi and Papa.

Trout fishing is my favorite thing to do with them and I'm pretty good at it. Mimi and Papa have an old cabin up in the mountains that used to belong to Mimi's parents, my great-grandparents who passed away before I was born. The three of us hike down into this canyon

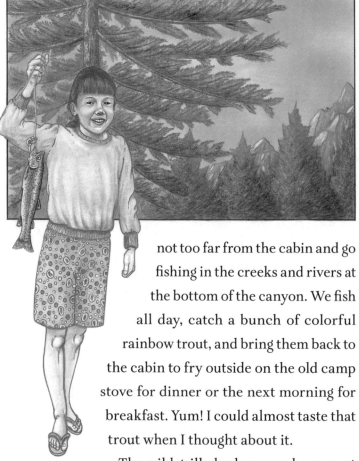

not too far from the cabin and go fishing in the creeks and rivers at the bottom of the canyon. We fish all day, catch a bunch of colorful rainbow trout, and bring them back to the cabin to fry outside on the old camp stove for dinner or the next morning for breakfast. Yum! I could almost taste that trout when I thought about it.

The wild grilled salmon we have up at Mimi and Papa's new house is pretty delicious too. Fresh fish seems to be the number one favorite food that everyone in my family likes best.

As I was daydreaming about that grilled salmon, I also remembered what we had for dessert after dinner that night—fresh blackberry pie made from what we'd foraged from the wild berry patches around Mimi and Papa's house.

Their house is on an island in the Puget Sound— totally different from the tropical islands I'm used to. Instead of palm trees, they live in a forest of huge pine trees. Instead of giant sea turtles, they have families of raccoons who stare at you like little bandits from up in the trees or along the driveway. Sometimes they even get bold enough to come up and stare at you through the dining room windows! And they really are little bandits. They love to steal the blackberries when they're just ripe for the picking. Luckily, there are enough berries to go around. We picked more than enough to bake our pie.

I've been making pie crust with Mimi for as long as I can remember. I think it was the first thing I ever learned how to bake. She let me make the pie dough by myself that day while she got the berries ready. I decided to let her roll out the chilled dough, because she's kind of picky about not wanting it handled too much.

After we lined the bottom of the pie pan with the rolled-out dough, we spooned in the berry mixture. Then we made a lattice top by weaving strips of dough over the top of the berries, which is just like weaving one of those potholders I used to make when I was small. The last thing I did was fold the edge of the bottom crust up and around the rim of the pie pan to make the little flutes or scallops. (Mimi calls it "crimping.") And then into the oven it went. That fresh wild blackberry pie was the perfect ending to our grilled salmon dinner.[5]

I supposed I could mention something about Mimi's pie crust in my essay. Even though we don't have wild blackberry pie during the Christmas holiday, we do make pumpkin and cherry pies. And my mom and I make pie crust just like Mimi does. At least that's one tradition I could write about.

Now, I was feeling hungry again. I wished more than anything that I had a piece of that blackberry pie.

---

5 It's a pretty amazing ending to any dinner! Try it out yourself— you can find the recipe on pages 104-109.

Chapter 6

Just as I climbed down the ladder to go look for something to eat, I heard Mom and Billy pull up in the driveway. I walked into the living room as they opened the front door.

"Finished?" they asked at the same time as they walked in.

"Not even," I answered. "I've got lots of ideas for a bunch of other topics, but I can't seem to come up with anything worth writing about how we celebrate our Christmas holiday."

"Aren't Lily and Maya going to be here pretty soon?" my mom asked. "And don't they have the same assignment? Maybe you can get some ideas from them. Your dad and I thought we could all go to Rosita's for tacos tonight instead of cooking. What do you think?"

I nodded enthusiastically, first of all because I was starving, and second, because I desperately needed to get out of the house and do something.

My friends arrived and we all piled into the car and headed down to the harbor to Rosita's, one of my favorite restaurants. It's such a cool place. They make fresh tacos and they're most famous for their catch-of-the-day fish tacos. You wait in line, cafeteria-style, place your order, and then you go to their salsa bar, where they have about a dozen different kinds of homemade salsas, from mild tomatillo to one so hot it will make you cry! The salsa bar also has cilantro, radishes, guacamole, and pickled onions and jalapeños. Next to the salsa bar there's a counter with these gigantic glass jars of *aguas frescas,* which are yummy drinks made with water and sugar mixed with fruit, flowers, rice, spices, and sometimes nuts. You can get *jugo de tamarindo* (tamarind juice), *horchata* (this tasty, milky drink made from ground almonds and rice with cinnamon and vanilla), or *agua de Jamaica* (hibiscus tea). I usually go for the *horchata.* There are tables that look out over the harbor and the bay, and sometimes you can see otters swimming and playing down below. We lucked out and got to see a mom with her newborn otter pup snuggling on her belly right below where we were sitting.

When we got back to the house after dinner, Lily and Maya wanted to watch *The Empire Strikes Back* for the hundred thousandth time. As Luke and Leia watched Lando fly away in search of Han Solo, we figured it was time to head upstairs and lay out the sleeping bags before we all fell asleep on the sofa in the family room.

Lily was the first one to wake up Sunday morning. She's the first one to do just about everything, including homework assignments. She's so annoying that way! She never has to study, she has a photographic memory, and she can just sit down and start writing about anything without even trying. She can also get ready to go somewhere in about two minutes and she always looks perfect. Like right then. Both she and Maya were awake and almost ready to go downstairs for breakfast, their naturally straight hair looking exactly like it did when we went to sleep.

Me, on the other hand? My curly hair looks like a giant poodle head when I wake up. It takes forever to brush out the tangles, and then I have to get it wet, pile on anti-frizz gel, and attempt to tame it . . . until I go outside in the foggy air, and then it turns into a frizz ball all over again. Usually I end up pulling it back into a ponytail, braiding it, or just pulling it up into a granny bun on top of my head. I decided to just go with the tangles so I wouldn't lag behind my friends.

"What's for breakfast?" Maya asked, already out of her sleeping bag and halfway dressed.

Lily finished getting dressed first, as usual. "Got any avocados?" she chimed in, along with a request for one of my special breakfasts: scrambled eggs (freshly laid by our backyard chickens) and avocado toast on that great sourdough French bread.

"I'll see how many eggs Mom has in the refrigerator and then we can go out in the backyard and collect some more from whatever the hens laid this morning," I told them.

"Awesome!" they both squealed, cheering and clapping their hands like we were going on the most excellent adventure of all time.

I don't think anyone else in the city limits has chickens in their backyard except for my crazy family. I'm usually kind of embarrassed by it, but I was kind of proud that morning to be able to offer fresh eggs to my sleepover guests—straight out of the henhouse and into the pan!

"Good morning, girls," my mom called out from the kitchen below.

"Morning, Mom," they hollered back.

"Ariel, are you going to make breakfast for your friends this morning, or shall I?"

"Thanks, Mom," I shouted down the ladder, "but I think I'll make scrambled eggs and avocado toast for everyone. How many eggs do we have in the fridge? And we DO have avos, right?"

"Six eggs in the fridge, and we ALWAYS have avocados," she answered, which was true. We never seemed to run out. My mom has been making me avocado toast for breakfast for as long as I can remember, maybe starting back in Colombia.

We took turns backing down the ladder, then headed out to the yard with my Shar-Pei, Coco, trotting along behind us. Billy was out there working on his bike.

"Good morning! Did you look for eggs yet?" I asked him, hoping he hadn't beaten us to the job.

"Not yet," he answered. "Go for it!"

Lily and Maya both greeted Billy, then we grabbed the egg basket off its hook on the fence and ran over to the chicken coop to look for eggs. My dad had already let the hens out of their house and into the yard for their daily exercise. They just went clucking along, not paying any attention to us as we set off to loot their nests.

Four new eggs: three light brown ones from the Barred Rock hens and one white one from the big White Leghorn, the hen my cousin Harry named "Double Chicken." Score! With these new eggs and the other six my mom had in the kitchen, there was enough for me to make scrambled eggs for everyone.

We carried the eggs back to the house and the girls plopped down at the little kitchen table while I started whipping up the breakfast I love to make. It's easy, quick, and yummy.[6]

"Can I do anything?" Maya offered.

"No thanks, I got it," I said, like I always do. "But, on second thought, you COULD set the table."

There's one thing about cooking—I don't like anyone

_____

6   I swear, it's so delicious and so simple—check out my foolproof recipe on pages 110-111.

to get in my way in the kitchen. If a recipe calls for a bunch of ingredients, I'll let my mom help me prep, because she knows what she's doing and I don't have to explain every step. Cooking, I like; teaching . . . not so much. Slicing up a few avocados, I asked Mom to make toast while I worked on the eggs.

There's really not much to making scrambled eggs, especially when you have fresh eggs from your own chickens. They taste so amazing, you don't have to add anything other than butter, salt, a little pepper, and maybe a little cream if you like.

I started melting butter in my mom's big frying pan while I cracked open all of the eggs and whisked them lightly in the mixing bowl. Once the butter got foamy, I poured the eggs into the pan and stirred them very gently with a wooden spoon until they started to set. I added a little bit of cream, stirred it in, and took the pan off the stove. I let the eggs finish cooking for a few seconds in the pan, but not for too long, so they wouldn't get rubbery. I sprinkled some sea salt and a bit of pepper on top.

My mom had finished making the sourdough toast,

Lily and Maya had set the table, and now all I had to do was squish a few slices of avocado a little bit with a fork on each piece of toast to spread them around, drizzle some olive oil over them, sprinkle on some sea salt and lemon pepper, line them up on a wooden serving board, and *voila!* Breakfast was ready. Mom grabbed a pitcher of orange juice from the fridge while I spooned the eggs onto a platter. We called my dad to come in, and we all sat down at the dining room table, ready to chow down.

Before we started serving ourselves, Lily commented about how I had arranged everything perfectly on the table. "It's like we're in a restaurant," she kidded.

"Yeah, I would have just made everyone come into the kitchen, pick up their own plate, grab a piece of toast off the counter and scoop up some eggs from the pan," Maya added.

We all laughed. My friends think I'm kind of weird—not just because I like to cook, but also because I like to make the food look beautiful when it's served. I must have learned that from Mom and my Mimi. Or maybe from all of my mom's cooking magazines. Probably a little bit of both. It's kind of like creating a piece of art. I guess I am a little weird, but no one seems to mind when I put the plate down in front of them.

As we were finishing breakfast, I finally took a deep breath and asked my friends if they were done writing their essays. I hadn't wanted to bring the subject up, but I was beginning to worry about getting my own assignment done in time for school the next day.

Maya said she just had to work a tiny bit on her ending.

"I finished mine on Friday night," Lily bragged.

Of course she did.

I knew they wanted me to go to the movies with them in the afternoon, but there was no way I could go. I couldn't believe I had to spend the whole rest of the day trying to write this impossible essay while my friends would be off enjoying a matinee.

My mom just couldn't help herself and had to ask, "Lily, what did you write about?"

Lily proceeded to tell us all about her Italian Christmas, which actually turned out to be kind of cool and interesting—unlike mine. Her Christmas goes on for a whole month—from St. Nicholas Day on

December 6th, when kids write letters to *San Nicolo* asking for presents and then leave their shoes out to be filled with small gifts, all the way to January 6th, the day of Epiphany (or *Día de los Reyes Magos*, Three Kings' Day, as my Mexican friends call it). That's when they celebrate the three wise men's visit to the Baby Jesus. On the night of January 5th, or the eve before the day of Epiphany, Italian kids put their stockings out and get gifts the next morning from this old witch lady, who they call *La Befana*. *La Befana* comes with a sack full of gifts, even after the children already got presents under the tree on Christmas Eve from Father Christmas,

which I guess is what they call Santa. (In Italian, it's *Babbo Natale*.) Kind of like a blend of Halloween and Christmas, which I think is pretty rad, especially since I was born on Halloween.

"No wonder you just powered through your essay," I whined, in true Hogan style. "You had so many things to write about that nobody has even heard of."

She just laughed and asked if I was close to finishing mine and if I'd be done in time to go to the movies.

"I don't think so," I told her, getting more frustrated by the minute. "I guess you guys are just going to have to go without me."

Everybody gave me the pity face.

"No big deal, I didn't really feel like sitting in a movie theater today anyway," I lied. "I'll just work on my essay for a few hours this afternoon and I should be done by dinner."

The girls helped clear the table and went upstairs to gather their things. Lily's mom arrived a few minutes later to pick them up and take them downtown to their matinee.

I felt like screaming after we said our goodbyes. I

was finally desperate enough to resort to asking my mom for help, which I almost never do!

"Why is it that I have more grandparents than anyone I know, they're all special and different in their own ways, but none of them has passed on one single holiday tradition? Why don't we have any culture?" I groaned.

Mom gave me one of those looks like a teacher who is about to teach you a lesson. "You know what? If you'll ride with me out to the farm to pick up our mystery box, I'll tell you a little bit about our family heritage and where our Christmas traditions come from."

Mariquita Farm is our friends' organic farm; we get boxes with different kinds of lettuces, fruits, and vegetables from them every other week. I got to work with them a few times, helping sell their organic produce up at the big farmers' market at the Ferry Building in San Francisco on Saturdays. That was really cool. But then they started delivering fruit and produce directly to restaurants and stopped selling at the farmers' market, so they decided to put together the mystery boxes for their regular customers who used to come every Saturday. When it's a mystery box week, Mom doesn't plan our Sunday dinner until she knows what we've got in the box. One thing is pretty certain—we are always going to have her everything-but-the-kitchen-sink salad. That's her thing, and it always contains produce from the farm.

I agreed to ride with her, wondering what kind of winter vegetables we would get along with the usual lettuce and hoping she might be able to finally give me some ideas for my essay.

Chapter 7

As we made our way out to the farm, which is close to my school, my mom reminded me that her family on her mom's side had come here from Europe four generations ago, most from Germany and some from Ireland, and that Grandpa Rich's family immigrated here from Germany and England. She said that this country has always been a nation of immigrants, but back when some of her ancestors came here, there were more people coming from Europe than anyplace else.

"Well, I should say that we are a nation made up of immigrants who came to a land that was already inhabited; we practically wiped out the indigenous peoples who lived here before the Europeans arrived. You know that where we live used to belong to Mexico, but before that, the land was populated by Native American tribes." She shook her head and continued, "And you can't call African American slaves immigrants, since they obviously didn't migrate here by choice. They were kidnapped from their homelands and brought here as property."

I was wondering where she was going with this history lesson and how it would help me understand my own culture.

"My point is, nowadays there are immigrants arriving from all corners of the globe, and they bring cultural contributions that make our country a much richer, more diverse and interesting place than it was back in my ancestors' time. Unfortunately, much of what you learn in school, what you read in literature, and who and what you see represented in movies and on television is still very one-sided, with an overemphasis on European culture."

My eyes started to glaze over—not because I disagreed with what she was saying, but because I had heard this speech so many times before. "Mom, I know all of this," I interrupted. "But you said you were going to tell me a little bit about our family heritage and where our Christmas traditions come from!"

"Oh, right," she agreed, "I got a little off track. I wanted to talk about the origins of how we celebrate, including how we decorate and what we eat and drink."

She talked about our Christmas tree decorations and how many of the antique glass ornaments we put on the tree every year were passed down from her grandparents, my great-grandparents, and how they were originally made in Germany. She told me this crazy story about when her mom, my Mimi, was a little girl and how she and her brother and sister would go to bed on Christmas Eve in a house that didn't have a single Christmas decoration on display. Mimi's parents, my great-grandparents, would wait for the kids to fall asleep, and then they would sneak a freshly cut Christmas tree into the house, completely decorate it, hang stockings by the fireplace, put out wooden nutcracker dolls, little pinecone trees decorated with miniature ornaments, and angel chimes with little candles—all while the kids were sleeping. Mimi and her brother and sister would wake up on Christmas morning to a magical wonderland that hadn't been there when they'd gone to bed the night before, complete with presents under the tree and stockings overflowing with goodies. I was definitely impressed! But I don't think I would be patient enough to wait until Christmas morning before doing one single Christmas activity. And I for sure can't imagine Mom and Billy doing all that by themselves in the middle of the night!

"So, now you know where our Christmas tree ornaments, our nutcrackers, our little pinecone trees and our angel chimes come from. My mom, Mimi, always used to tell me the story about those angel chimes that spin around by the power of the candle flames and how they represent an old Christmas Eve legend. The legend says that bells throughout the world are rung by angels announcing the birth of the Baby Jesus. All of these are German traditions, as is the idea of decorating an evergreen tree in the first place. You know that Christmas song, *O Tannenbaum*? That's German for 'fir tree' or 'pine tree', but the song has come to represent the Christmas tree. And you know your Advent calendar, where you open the little doors counting down the twenty-four days leading to Christmas? That was made in Germany too, and was first used by the German Lutherans. Exchanging Christmas gifts was symbolic for the wise men bringing gifts to the Baby Jesus, but then morphed into the commercialized Christmas shopping frenzy that it is today—that also has roots in the traditions of shopping for gifts in the German Christmas markets."

I listened and pictured all of the familiar decorations I've grown up with—I'd never realized they were connected to German traditions. I was surprised Mom never told me this story before. It's hard to imagine myself being connected to German culture in any way. I can accept that I'm not Mexican after all, but German? I can just imagine myself dressed in a traditional *dirndl*, like the ones my mom's cousin Kay loves to wear. Her mom was actually born and raised in Germany and didn't come to this country until she was grown, so I know that those cousins really are part German.

"Ok, I get that a lot of our decorations come from Germany, but what about our Christmas Eve dinner and our Christmas morning breakfast? What about the crab *cioppino* you always make, the frozen peaches and apricot strudel we have every Christmas morning, the eggnog, the sparkling cider, the pies, the Christmas cookies?" I started to sound a little frantic, and not at all

ready to write an essay about being German.

"Hold those thoughts," Mom said as we arrived at the farm. "Let's go pick up our mystery box, and then we can talk about food on the way home."

Mom called our box "Purple Haze" when she saw it. It was full of all kinds of pretty purple things: purple speckled radicchio, purple daikon radishes, purple romaine lettuce, and purple baby carrots.

"All we need to add is some roasted pecans, a little pecorino cheese, a balsamic vinaigrette, and we've got the fixings for a great salad!" she exclaimed. "We can swing by the market and pick up a rotisserie chicken on the way home and we'll be all set for dinner."

On our drive back to the house, Mom gave me the history of the funny mix of things that have turned into my family's traditional Christmas foods. She started with the crab *cioppino*: "It might seem strange that our Christmas Eve tradition consists of a classic Italian-American dish, seeing as how we don't have a drop of Italian blood anywhere in our family."

She reminded me that her mom, my Mimi, moved to the San Francisco Bay Area when she was about my age. She lived in an Italian neighborhood and had lots of Italian-American friends in school.

Mimi tells me stories about her teenage years, and I crack up when she tells me the names of some of the guys she used to date before she met Grandpa Rich (and definitely before she met Papa)—Tito Tosti, Berto Bacigalupi, Bruno Bonucci, and Luigi Panicucci. She's not making fun of them, it's just that the sounds of their last names rhyme, which sends me into hysterics every time. I hadn't thought of that for a long time; I made a note to myself that I needed to share that story with Lily.

Mom explained, "Dungeness crab is in season here and in the Bay Area around Christmas time, so that's when the people Mimi grew up with used to make the delicious seafood and fish stew we know as crab *cioppino*. Mimi's mom, your great-grandmother, learned how to make it, Mimi learned it from her, and I learned how to make it from Mimi. I can teach you how to make it this year if you'd like, and it will be a fourth-generation recipe. That's what I'd call tradition!"

I liked that idea, and it made me think about how

cultural traditions can be passed down in your family. Your ancestors don't have to come from Italy for you to like to cook Italian food, or Mexico for you to like to cook Mexican food, or France for you to like to make *escargot*. My mom's ancestors came from Germany, but that didn't mean that she only has German cultural traditions or that she only cooks German food. Billy grew up eating a lot of southern soul food with his family in Jersey, but he's lived here for so long that now he's totally a local dude; he eats more organic veggies and *burritos al pastor* than anyone I know!

"Mom, do you even know how to cook anything German?"

"Well, let me think for a minute . . . I don't really do much German cooking, although the apricot strudel we have on Christmas morning is actually a German recipe that also comes from my grandma, your great-grandma."

"And the frozen peaches?"

Mom laughed and explained that the frozen peaches are a carryover from her own childhood. She and her brothers, my uncles, used to go with Mimi and Papa to buy fresh peaches in the summer when they drove back from their grandparents' cabin. They would stop at roadside stands in the Central Valley and buy crates of these sweet, juicy, fresh-from-the-orchard peaches, and then when they got home, Mimi would peel them, slice them, put them in storage bags, and stick them in the freezer to enjoy later in the winter months. Christmas morning was one of those winter days when the frozen peaches would come out. Mom decided she liked that tradition, so she buys fresh peaches in the summer at farmers' markets and freezes them just like Mimi. And that's why we have frozen peaches on Christmas morning with our apricot strudel. They still have a little bit of icy peach juice slush when we eat them and they taste way better than canned peaches. I think they might even taste better than fresh peaches!

Our Christmas dinners seem to be different every year. We don't have a particular meal that's passed down from grandparents or anything. I don't even know what we are having this Christmas. Sometimes it can be prime rib, sometimes it's lamb, some years we have steak, and some years we have salmon. The only other things we have on a regular basis are Christmas cookies, pumpkin and cherry pies, eggnog (which I found out is my great-grandfather's recipe), and sparkling apple cider that comes from local apples—nothing all that special to add to an essay.

On our way home, we stopped by our local market to pick up the rotisserie chicken. Walking from the car to the store, I glanced up at two of the murals painted on the sides of the market and the building next to it. One is of a big whale out in the bay and a scene from Lighthouse Point with surfers catching waves at "The Lane;" the other mural, I hadn't ever really paid attention to before. The words are written in Spanish, and even though I can translate them to English, I hadn't thought that much about what the expression meant. *Dime lo que comes y te diré quién eres*: "Tell me what you eat, and I will tell you who you are."

I stopped for a second and thought about how that related to all the things I'd been thinking about over the weekend. But then I ran ahead to catch up with my mom.

By the time we got back to the house, made Mom's

everything-but-the-kitchen-sink salad,[7] and sat down to eat our Sunday dinner, the sun had already set. There weren't that many hours left in my weekend.

Once we finished eating, I asked if I could be excused from the table so I could go back up to my room and try to write my essay before I nodded out. I really only had three choices: finish the essay that night, set my alarm for 4:00 a.m. and try to finish before we left for school in the morning, or fake a stomachache and try to convince my mom to let me stay home for the day. Staying home sick wouldn't even have been a lie—my stomach really was doing flip flops the more anxious I got about my task!

---

7   It's such a delicious and healthy dinner—check out pages 112-114 and try it for yourself!

Chapter 8

I climbed back up in my loft, walked over to my desk, and read the things I had written on the chart. My mind circled around and around, thinking about everyone in my family, all the food memories, all the different places I've been, all of the different traditions . . . but mostly about how my culture just didn't fit into a five-paragraph essay about holiday cultural traditions. To describe anything about my family's cultural contributions, I felt like I needed to include all the experiences of my life that make me who I am 365 days a year.

The words from that mural popped back into my head. *Dime lo que comes y te diré quién eres.* "Tell me what you eat, and I will tell you who you are."

Suddenly, a new idea came flooding into my brain. It was like Yoda himself appeared in my room and gave me a clue and I was finally awakened to the Force! Ok, maybe that's a little dramatic, but I felt like someone was shining a spotlight in my room; I saw things more clearly than I ever had before.

"Forget about a CHRISTMAS essay!" I said out loud.

My teacher never actually said it had to be about Christmas—just about holiday traditions. My traditions are spread across all four seasons and they come from lots of different parts of the world!

I moved my chart pad onto the bed, then pulled my chair up to the desk and sat down. I picked up my notebook, took out my colored pencils, and I drew a quick sketch of that mural with its Spanish saying. I wrote the English translation underneath it.

And then, just like magic, I began to write. The words flowed as fast as I could get them on paper. Before I knew it, a poem emerged:

Girl of Four Seasons

In the Spring, I'm an organic girl
From farm and market and yard
Strawberries, radishes, arugula,
Asparagus, leeks, and chard.

In the Summer, I'm an island girl
Where the fish and fruit are best
From Hawaii to the Caribbean
And up to the Pacific Northwest.

In the Fall, I'm a local girl
Homegrown in the Monterey Bay
Apples, mussels, and Brussels sprouts
Fish tacos and salsa all day.

In the Winter, I'm a European girl
Family recipes come from afar
Cioppino[8], strudel, and eggnog
What we eat is who we are.

---

8   It's a more complicated recipe than most of the others I've shared
with you, but the story of my holiday traditions wouldn't be complete
without instructions for making your own crab *cioppino*—find it on
pages 115-117!

Freckle-Faced Foodie Recipes

Recipe: Mimi's Fresh Basil Pesto with Bowtie Pasta (Chapter 1)

Makes 4 - 6 servings

INGREDIENTS

1/3 cup pine nuts, lightly toasted

2 cups fresh basil leaves, washed and packed (without the
stems)

3 cloves garlic, peeled

1/3 cup parmesan cheese, grated (fresh, if possible)

1/2 cup extra-virgin olive oil

Sea salt to taste

Pepper to taste

1 lb. dried Italian farfalle pasta (bowtie pasta)

INSTRUCTIONS

1. Heat a frying pan over medium-high heat
and toast the pine nuts until they
are golden, stirring them
occasionally.

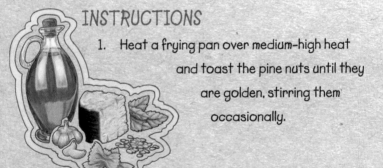

2. Put the toasted pine nuts in the bowl of a small food processor, along with the basil leaves, the garlic cloves, and the parmesan cheese.

3. Pulse until everything is finely chopped. (You might have to scrape the sides down with a small spatula as pieces fly away from the blade.)

4. With the food processor running, slowly add the olive oil in a thin stream until the oil and the other ingredients are well combined. Keep scraping down the sides of the food processor bowl with the spatula.

5. Season with salt and pepper to taste.

6. Follow the directions on the pasta bag or box to cook all of the pasta, then pour the cooked pasta into a colander to drain all the water out.

7. Toss about half a cup of the basil pesto with the pasta. You'll probably have some pesto left over—it's great to spread on toast the next morning!

8. Divide into 4 - 6 bowls and sprinkle a little more parmesan cheese on top.

Recipe: Nana Fox's Patacones
(Chapter 2)

Makes 4 servings

INGREDIENTS

2 - 4 plantains, very green
Salted water
Vegetable oil or coconut oil
Sea salt

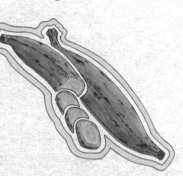

INSTRUCTIONS

1. When opening a plantain, the peel is really hard. You
   have to cut 1/4" off of each end of the plantain (the
   tips), then slice along each of the lines of the body to
   go through the peel—but you don't want to slice up the
   fruit inside. Once you have sliced along each line, you will
   be able to peel it easily.

2. Slice each peeled plantain into 1 1/2" slices.

3. Place the sliced plantains in a big bowl of salted water
   that tastes as salty as the sea, and soak them for
   about 20 minutes.

4. Take the slices out, place them on paper towels, and blot them until they are dry.

5. Heat up about 1" of the oil in a frying pan on medium heat until hot.

6. Fry the plantain slices on both sides for about 3 minutes, or until they are golden. You may have to do this in batches because you don't want the slices to be crowded in the pan. Best to use tongs to turn the slices over, and be very careful not to splash yourself with the hot oil!

7. When they are golden, remove them from the pan with a slotted spoon and place them on a plate covered with paper towels to soak up the oil.

8. Put each fried plantain on a cutting board and smash or flatten it with the bottom of a glass until it is about 1/4" thick.

9. Place the flattened plantains in the hot oil again and fry until both sides are golden brown.

10. Take them out again with a slotted spoon and drain them on paper towels.

11. Sprinkle with sea salt.

12. Serve immediately.

Recipe: Aloha Smoothie
(Chapter 3)

Makes 4 servings

INGREDIENTS

1 large ripe papaya

1 large or 2 small ripe, but still firm, mango(s)—more yellow
   than green or red

1/2 cup orange juice

1/2 cup milk

4 ice cubes

1 tablespoon honey (if you want it to be sweeter)

INSTRUCTIONS

1. Cut the papaya in half and scoop out the seeds.
2. Cut the peel off the halves, chop the peeled papaya into
   chunks, and place in a blender.
3. Holding the mango with one hand, stand it on its end,
   stem side down. With a sharp knife in your other hand,
   carefully cut from the top of the mango down one side
   of the flat pit in the center. Then repeat on the other

side. You should end up with three pieces: two halves, and a middle section that includes the pit.

4. Take one of the mango halves and use a knife to make crisscross cuts in it (lengthwise and crosswise), but try not to cut through the peel. Turn the mango half inside out so that the cut pieces are sticking out like a hedgehog. Cut away the small square pieces with a paring knife and place them in the blender. Repeat with the other half. There will be some yummy mango left on the seed . . . this is for the chef! Don't let it go to waste!

5. Cover the fruit in the blender with the orange juice and milk (and optional honey).

6. Add the ice cubes and blend until very smooth.

7. Pour into four glasses.

Recipe: Nana's Sweet Potato Pudding (Chapter 4)

Makes 8 servings

INGREDIENTS

2 lbs. sweet potatoes (about 6 medium)

1 cup light brown sugar, packed

4 tablespoons butter (1/4 cup or 1/2 stick)

1 can evaporated milk (5 oz.)

3 eggs, lightly beaten

1 teaspoon vanilla extract

1/2 teaspoon ground cinnamon

1/2 teaspoon ground nutmeg

Whipped cream

INSTRUCTIONS

1. Peel the sweet potatoes with a potato peeler and cut them into 1" cubes.

2. Place the potatoes in a medium-sized pot and cover them with water. Bring the water to a boil and cook

for 15 to 20 minutes, or until the potatoes are tender enough to push a fork through.

3. Pour the potatoes into a colander and drain them. Let them cool a bit and then put them into a large mixing bowl along with the butter and mash well with a potato masher.

4. Preheat the oven to 350° and lightly spray a 2-quart baking dish with nonstick baking spray.

5. Stir the mashed sweet potatoes and butter together with the brown sugar, evaporated milk, eggs, vanilla extract, cinnamon, and nutmeg until they are well mixed.

6. Pour the mixture into the baking dish and bake for about 45 minutes or until a knife inserted in the center comes out clean.

7. Cool and then refrigerate.

8. Serve with whipped cream on top (fresh or from the can).

Recipe: Mimi's Wild Blackberry Pie
(Chapter 5)

Makes 1 pie

INGREDIENTS FOR THE WILD BLACKBERRY PIE FILLING

- 5 - 6 cups blackberries, ripe, rinsed, picked clean, and patted dry
- 1/2 - 3/4 cup sugar
- 1 teaspoon fresh lemon juice
- 1 teaspoon lemon zest (from the peel of the lemon, grated with a microplane or zester)
- 1/2 teaspoon ground cinnamon
- 4 tablespoons cornstarch or flour

INSTRUCTIONS FOR MAKING THE PIE FILLING

1. Place the blackberries, sugar, lemon juice, lemon zest, cinnamon, and cornstarch or flour in a large mixing bowl.
2. Very gently fold in the berries in a rolling motion until they are well coated with the mixture.
3. Put the bowl aside while you make the pie crust.

INGREDIENTS FOR PIE CRUST MADE IN A FOOD PROCESSOR (2 CRUSTS, TOP AND BOTTOM)

3 cups all-purpose flour (spooned into the measuring cup and leveled off with a knife)

2 teaspoons sugar

1 teaspoon salt

1/2 cup chilled, unsalted butter (1 stick)

1/2 cup cold vegetable shortening

1/2 cup ice water

INSTRUCTIONS FOR MAKING THE DOUGH

1. Cut the butter in 1/2" slices and put them in the refrigerator while you prepare the flour mixture.

2. Place the flour, sugar, and salt in the bowl of a food processor with a steel blade and pulse it a few times to mix.

3. Take the butter from the refrigerator and add it to the flour mixture in the food processor bowl, along with the cold shortening, and pulse 8 to 12 times, until the butter is the size of peas.

4. Drizzle the ice water in a slow stream down the feed tube of the food processor and pulse the machine until the dough begins to form a ball.

5. Dump the ball out onto a floured surface (like a cutting board, counter, or pastry cloth), roll it into a smoother ball, wrap it in plastic wrap, and refrigerate it for 30 minutes.

6. Take the ball of dough out, cut it in half, and put one half back in the refrigerator.

INSTRUCTIONS FOR ROLLING OUT THE BOTTOM CRUST

1. Flatten the half of the ball left on your floured surface once with the palm of your hand and then roll it out on the floured surface into a 13" circle. Be sure to roll from the center to the edge, turning and flouring the dough so it doesn't stick to the surface. Try not to handle it too much!

2. Fold the dough in half, carefully place it into a 12" pie pan (a non-stick pan or a greased pan) without stretching it at all, and unfold it to fit the pan.

3. Carefully cut the dough with a paring knife so that it is hanging evenly over the pan by about 1/2" and then fold the edge under so it is laying on top of the lip of the pie pan all the way around and crimp the edges with your fingers.

4. Chill in the refrigerator while you roll out and prepare the lattice top.

5. Preheat the oven to 400º.

INSTRUCTIONS FOR ROLLING OUT THE TOP LATTICE CRUST

1. Take the second ball of dough out of the refrigerator, flatten it with your palm, and roll it on the floured surface into a 13" circle. Be sure to roll from the center to the edge, turning and flouring the dough so it doesn't stick to the surface.
2. Cut your pie crust circle into 1" strips (you can use a ruler!) with a knife or a pizza cutter.
3. Leave the cut strips in the circle because they will help you know where to place them on the pie.

INSTRUCTIONS FOR PUTTING THE PIE TOGETHER

First, you take the pie pan with the bottom crust inside of it out of the refrigerator and spoon the wild blackberry mixture into it. Next, you take the strips of dough that you just cut and weave them over the top of the berry-filled pie pan. If you've ever woven a potholder, you'll know exactly how to do this when you see all of the strips of dough cut out and ready to go. An easier way to do this is to make a "faux" lattice top by following these steps:

1. Lay half of the strips vertically across the top of the berry mix, leaving a little space in between each strip. Make sure they're evenly spaced.
2. Lay the other half of the strips horizontally (and evenly) across the vertical strips, which makes the top look like it's woven once it bakes in the oven, even though it isn't actually woven. That's why it's called a "faux" lattice top—"faux" means "fake."
3. Fold under any strip edges that are hanging over the pan, tucking them inside of the crimped bottom crust.

INSTRUCTIONS FOR BAKING THE PIE

1. Bake the pie in two stages. First, bake it at 400º for 30 minutes.
2. Then, place a sheet of aluminum foil loosely over the pie to protect the edges and lattice top from getting too burnt, reduce the temperature to 350º and bake for another 20-25 minutes, or until the crust has browned and the filling is bubbly.
3. Remove the pie from the oven and place it on a wire cooling rack and let it cool completely before slicing it.

Recipe: Scrambled Eggs in Butter with Avocado Toast (Chapter 6)

Makes 4 - 6 servings

INGREDIENTS FOR AVOCADO TOAST

4 - 6 slices sourdough bread, toasted

2 - 3 just-ripe avocados

Extra-virgin olive oil to drizzle

Sea salt to taste

Lemon pepper to taste

INSTRUCTIONS FOR AVOCADO TOAST

1. Peel the avocado, take the seed out, and cut the fruit into 1/2" slices.
2. Toast the bread slices.
3. Place the avocado slices to cover each piece of toast and gently smoosh them with a fork.
4. Drizzle olive oil over each piece of toast and sprinkle sea salt and lemon pepper on top.

INGREDIENTS FOR SCRAMBLED EGGS

8 - 10 fresh, organic eggs laid by free-range hens—best if
the hens just laid them!

3 tablespoons unsalted butter

1/4 cup whole milk, half and half, or heavy cream

Sea salt to taste

Ground pepper to taste

INSTRUCTIONS FOR SCRAMBLED EGGS

1. In a medium mixing bowl, lightly beat the eggs with a fork
   or whisk.
2. Heat the butter in a non-stick frying pan over medium
   heat until it gets foamy.
3. Add the eggs and cook, stirring with a wooden spoon
   until they begin to set.
4. Gently stir in the milk, half and half, or cream and then
   immediately take the pan off the stove before the eggs
   get too cooked or rubbery.
5. Add sea salt and pepper to taste.

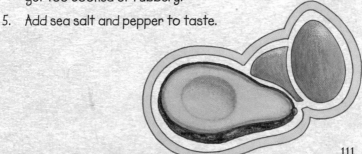

Recipe: My Mom's Everything-but-the-Kitchen-Sink Salad
With Balsamic Vinaigrette Dressing
(Chapter 7)

Makes 4 - 6 servings

INGREDIENTS FOR DRESSING

2 garlic cloves, peeled

A pinch of sea salt for the garlic paste

A pinch of sea salt for the dressing

1 tablespoon Dijon mustard

2 1/2 tablespoons balsamic vinegar

1/2 cup extra-virgin olive oil

Sea salt and freshly ground pepper to season the tossed
 salad

INSTRUCTIONS FOR DRESSING

1. Pound the garlic to a paste with the pinch of sea salt.
   You can use the back of a knife, a meat mallet, or best of
   all, a mortar and pestle.

2. In a small bowl, combine the garlic, mustard, balsamic vinegar, and the other pinch of sea salt.

3. Whisk in the olive oil and taste the dressing with a small piece of lettuce.

4. Adjust to taste with more vinegar, oil, or salt.

INGREDIENTS FOR SALAD

One head red leaf or other fresh lettuce (like romaine or Boston bibb), cleaned

1 1/2 cups arugula

1 cup radicchio

1/4 cup red onion, thinly sliced

1/4 cup cucumber, thinly sliced (peeled or unpeeled)

1 avocado, ripe, sliced and cut into bite-sized pieces

Any other sliced or chopped fresh vegetable or fruit you'd like to add (oven-roasted beets, tomatoes, carrots, bell peppers, radishes, apples, peaches, pears, etc.)

Toasted and chopped pecans or almonds (optional)

INSTRUCTIONS FOR SALAD

1. Rinse and dry the lettuce leaves, the arugula, and the radicchio in a salad spinner or between paper towel sheets.
2. Slice the red onion, cucumber, avocado, and other vegetables or fruits you'd like to add.
3. Just before serving the salad, put the greens and other vegetables or fruits (and the chopped nuts if you are adding those) in a large bowl, season with the salt and pepper, and gently toss (best with your hands!) with enough vinaigrette to coat the leaves lightly. Don't overdress. You can always add more, but you can't subtract!

Recipe: Mimi's Crab Cioppino
(Chapter 8)

Makes 6 servings

This is the most complicated recipe I'm sharing, but it's a very special one, made for a very special occasion. It has the most ingredients, but if you have someone to help you prep, it's not too difficult to make.

INGREDIENTS

1 large yellow onion, diced
1 bunch green onions, sliced
1 bell pepper, seeded and diced
3 whole cloves garlic, peeled
1/3 cup olive oil
1/3 cup parsley, chopped
1 can (16 oz.) tomato purée
1 can (8 oz.) tomato paste or sauce
1 tomato sauce can (8 oz.) filled with red or white wine
1 tomato sauce can (8 oz.) filled with water
1 bay leaf

3 teaspoons sea salt

1/4 teaspoon pepper

1/8 teaspoon rosemary

1/8 teaspoon thyme

2 medium Dungeness crabs, cracked and cleaned[1]

1 dozen fresh clams in shells

1 lb. prawns or large shrimp, cleaned and with the veins removed, but in their shells

1 lb. whitefish, cut into bite-sized pieces

INSTRUCTIONS

1. In a Dutch oven or any heavy-bottom braising pot, sauté the yellow onion, green onions, green pepper, and garlic in olive oil for about 5 minutes.

2. Add parsley, tomato purée, sauce, wine, water, and all seasonings.

3. Cover and simmer about one hour. Remove garlic.

4. Have someone help you clean and crack the crab, or have this done at the fish market where you buy the crab.

5. Scrub the clams well.

---

1 Dungeness crabs are very rarely available in most of the U.S., making this recipe truly San Francisco or Monterey Bay. If you're having trouble finding them, you could try using lobster tails as a substitute.

6. Wash the shrimp or prawns and remove the sand vein with the tip of a paring knife or other vein-removing tool. (My mom has a special tool for doing this.)

7. Place the shellfish into the sauce in the Dutch oven in this order: crab on the bottom, clams on top of crab, prawns or shrimp on top of clams.

8. Cover and simmer until the clamshells open, about 20-30 minutes. Add the whitefish and simmer for 5-8 more minutes.

9. Serve with French bread.

Buon appetito!

About the Authors

Ariel Fox is now an award-winning chef in New York City and a new mom raising her own little foodie. Long before her rise to the top of her field and her recent win as Gordon Ramsay's Hell's Kitchen 2019 top chef, she began her culinary path as a quirky young girl who happened to pay attention to the intricacies of food wherever she went. You can visit her on Instagram @chefarielfox.

Marlin Adams, in addition to being Ariel's mom, is an educator and former executive director of the California Reading and Literature Project for the University of California, where she published numerous curriculum guides and educational texts for language and literacy teachers. This is her first children's book, in which she vividly brings to life her daughter's childhood escapades in the kitchen. Marlin lives with her husband in Brooklyn, New York.

About the Illustrator

Luiz Homero Pereira is a Brazilian-American artist painting in the realist and surrealist style. While he has worked most of his life as an illustrator/graphic designer, this is his first collaboration on a children's book. He lived most of his life in Santa Cruz, California, but now resides with his wife in South Florida. He can be reached at dospampas2002@yahoo.com.